"If anyone deserves to get smitted, it's Eric!" Charlie argued.

"Smitten, not smitted," I said, "and nobody deserves to get smitten."

"... they do," said Zeus. "Anyway, ... easy way to solve a problem. ... minute there's a rotten kid going around eating my sacrifices and defiling my image, next minute there's a flash and a bang and a pair of smoking shoes. That'll show him!"

"... said Charlie. "Is *that* what ... means?"

"... course!" Zeus said. "In the old ... as always smiting people ... nderbolts. If I smote you, you ... tten. Once smitten, twice fi... that's what they used to say about my smitings—"

"Maybe," I interrupted, "but you can't go around smiting people in school. It's against the rules . . ."

Also by John Dougherty,
and published by Random House Children's Books:

In Young Corgi Books for primary readers:

ZEUS ON THE LOOSE!
'Energetic and page-turning' *INK magazine*
Shortlisted for the Branford Boase Award

ZEUS TO THE RESCUE
'Instantly involving, constantly hilarious . . . Zeus is a superb
character' Andy Stanton (author of *Mr Gum*), *Junior Education*

NITERACY HOUR
'Unique . . . a great example of the quirky humour that younger
readers enjoy' *Children's Books in Ireland*
Shortlisted for the Nottingham Children's Book Award

JACK SLATER, MONSTER INVESTIGATOR
'A clever story, cleverly told' *Carousel*
Shortlisted for the Ottaker's Children's Book Prize

JACK SLATER AND THE WHISPER OF DOOM
'A rollicking adventure . . . plot by the bucketload, an interesting
world to investigate, scary monsters, a snivelling rival, quirky
humour, lessons to be learned, and everyone's home again in
time for breakfast' *Bookbag*

In Corgi Yearling Books, for junior readers:

BANSI O'HARA AND THE BLOODLINE PROPHECY
'A highly entertaining read with plenty of comic relief to the
book's darker moments' *Carousel*
'A romping good read' *INIS*

BANSI O'HARA AND THE EDGES OF HALLOWE'EN
COMING SOON

For more information about John Dougherty:
www.visitingauthor.com

JoHn DouGHerTy

Zeus
Sorts it Out

Illustrated by Georgien Overwater

YOUNG CORGI

ZEUS SORTS IT OUT
A YOUNG CORGI BOOK 978 0 552 55807 5

Published in Great Britain by Young Corgi Books,
an imprint of Random House Children's Books
A Random House Group Company

This edition published 2011

1 3 5 7 9 10 8 6 4 2

The Random House Group Limited supports the Forest Stewardship
Council® (FSC®), the leading international forest certification organiation.
All our titles that are printed on Greenpeace approved FSC® certified paper carry
the FSC® logo. Our paper procurement policy can be found at
www.randomhouse.co.uk/environment

Set in 17/20pt Bembo Schoolbook
by Falcon Oast Graphic Art Ltd

Young Corgi Books are published by Random House Children's Books,
61–63 Uxbridge Road, London W5 5SA,

www.kidsatrandomhouse.co.uk
www.randomhouse.co.uk
www.totallyrandombooks.co.uk

Addresses for companies within The Random House Group Limited can
be found at: www.randomhouse.co.uk/offices.htm

THE RANDOM HOUSE GROUP Limited Reg. No. 954009

A CIP catalogue record for this book is available from the British Library.

Printed and bound in Great Britain by CPI Bookmarque, Croydon, CR0 4TD

As ever, first and foremost for Noah & Cara,
with all my love

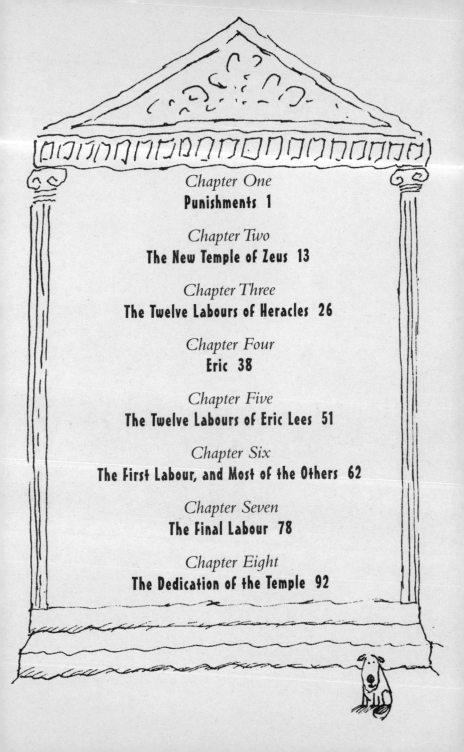

Chapter One

Punishments

This is me.

And this is the Greek god Zeus.

And this is the story of what happened when he met the school bully.

It all started
when Charlie
came into class
with a wet head.

"Charlie!" said
Miss Wise. "What
have you been
doing?"

"Um . . . I was
getting a drink
from the water
fountain, and I . . .
er . . . I pressed the button too hard,"
Charlie said. I could tell Miss Wise
wasn't convinced, but she didn't ask
him any more questions, and he came
and sat down beside me.

"You can't get your head wet
like that from the water fountain,"
I whispered to him when I had a
chance. "What really happened?"

"Um . . ." Charlie said again.

"Um . . . I got it wet in the toilets."

"What," I said, "you mean in the basin?"

"No," he said hesitantly. "Actually in the toilet."

I stared at him. "Did someone put your head down the toilet?" I asked.

Charlie suddenly looked scared. "No!" he said. "No! I . . . er . . . I did it myself."

I was so astonished I almost forgot to whisper. "Charlie, you idiot! What did you put your own head down the toilet for?" I asked.

"I didn't mean to," Charlie said. "I just . . . er . . . I just accidentally sat on the toilet upside down."

That didn't sound likely. Charlie can be a bit daft sometimes, but even he's not silly enough to forget which way up you're supposed to sit on the toilet.

"Come on, Charlie," I said. "You

can tell me who did it."

"I can't," he said miserably. "He said he'd kill me if I told anyone."

"Who did?" I asked.

"Eric," he said. Then he gasped, and clapped his hand to his mouth.

That made sense. Eric was the biggest, meanest, nastiest kid in the school, and everyone usually avoided him if they could. "Has he been bullying you all week?" I said. "Is that why you haven't had a play time snack for days?"

Charlie nodded glumly. "He's been taking my crisps off me before school starts. I went to the boys' toilets to try and hide from him today, but he found me, and . . ." His voice tailed off sadly, and he pointed at his wet head.

"What else has he been doing?" I asked.

"Hitting me, and tripping me, and calling me names. And . . . he did this too." Charlie took something out of his pocket and showed me. It was his new card game – one where each card has a different character on it, and they all have scores for things like strength and power and wisdom. Usually we're not allowed to bring that sort of game in, but Miss Wise had given Charlie special permission for this one because it was educational. All the characters were ancient Greek gods and heroes.

top card was Zeus. It was kind
favourite, because we knew
al Zeus – although the picture
wasn't a very good likeness. It made
him look all strong and noble and
heroic, whereas actually he looked
more like . . . well, a big bloke in a bed
sheet. And it gave him a score of nine
out of ten for wisdom, but considering
some of the daft things Zeus had done
when he'd come to our school before,
I didn't think he was very wise at all.
I'd have given him one out of ten. Or
maybe less.

Still, it was our favourite card.
But Eric had drawn
glasses on Zeus's
face, and flowers on
his tunic, and he'd
scribbled out all the
scores and given him
zero for everything.

6

And he'd crumpled it too. The card was ruined.

I didn't know what to say. But I didn't have a chance to say anything, because just then a hand touched my shoulder, very lightly, and Miss Wise said, "Stop talking, Alex. Put those cards away right now, Charlie. And if the two of you can't tell me something about Tartarus in five minutes' time, you can stay in and do your research at play time."

So we had to find out about
Tartarus instead of talking about Eric.

It was interesting, though. We
learned that the ancient Greeks
believed Tartarus was the place where
bad people went to get punished,
and we found out about some of the
people who got punished there.

There was
Ixion, who got
fastened to a big
burning wheel
that wouldn't stop
rolling around.

Then there was
Tantalus, who
had to stand in a river with bunches
of grapes above him. He was really
hungry and thirsty, but every time he
tried to pick some of the grapes they
rose up above him, and every time he
bent to drink from the river the water

level went down below him, so he could never quite reach them.

And then there was Sisyphus, who had to roll a huge rock up to the top of a big hill. Every time he got near the top the rock got away from him and rolled all the way back down and he had to start all over again.

We told Miss Wise all this when it was our turn to present our research, and it seemed to be enough for her. Or nearly enough; because just before she asked Sophie and Leah what they'd found out about naiads, she said to us:

"So, who was it who actually gave these bad people their punishments?"

"Was it their teachers, miss?" Troy shouted out. Everyone laughed.

Miss Wise ignored him, and looked at us with an expression that meant: *Well? I'm waiting.*

"Um . . ." Charlie said, and looked at me.

"Er . . . the gods?" I guessed.

"Well done, Alex," Miss Wise

said. "It was the gods. I wonder what punishment they'd think up for someone who kept calling out instead of listening," she added, looking at Troy, and everyone laughed again.

Everyone except Charlie. He had a thinking sort of expression on his face.

"Yeah," he said softly to himself. "Of course. The gods punished bad people . . ."

I should have known then that we were heading for trouble.

After we'd all talked about our research, we had a few minutes to choose an Ancient Greek Activity Sheet before the next lesson. I wanted to talk to Charlie about Eric, but he wouldn't; he just sat cutting and sticking something. So it wasn't until a bit later that I had the chance to whisper to him:

"Listen . . . about Eric . . ."

"Don't worry about Eric," he whispered back. "I'm going to sort him out good and proper."

I looked at him, puzzled. The other kids in Eric's own class hadn't been able to sort him out; I couldn't see Charlie managing. "How are you going to do that?" I said.

In answer, Charlie pulled something out of his pocket – something small and crumpled, and made of paper. I stared at it.

"Charlie," I began; and I was about to say, *How do you expect to sort Eric out with a badly made paper house?* when I realized. It wasn't a house. It was a temple.

Charlie was going to call for Zeus.

Chapter Two

The New Temple of Zeus

"Oh, no," I said. "Charlie, no. Things are bad enough without bringing Zeus back."

"He got us out of trouble last time," Charlie said.

"Yes, but he got us *into* most of that trouble in the first place! I nearly ended up spending the rest of my life as a pig! And the time before, we had to stop him starting a war in the playground!"

"Don't care," Charlie said moodily. "I'd rather be a pig than have Eric picking on me every day."

13

"Look," I said desperately, "I bet Zeus won't answer if you pray into that temple, anyway." I picked up the leftover scrap of Charlie's activity sheet. "See?" I said. "It says, *Build a Greek Temple*. Not a Temple of Zeus – just any old temple. It won't work if it isn't a Temple of Zeus."

"That's all you know," Charlie said. "Look!"

He showed me the bit he'd cut off from the bottom of the sheet. There was a whole paragraph there about how, after the ancient Greeks had built a temple, they dedicated it to the god they'd built it for.

"See?" he said. "I'll just dedicate it to Zeus, and then it'll be his temple, and then I can ask him to come and sort Eric out."

Sometimes I think people like Charlie shouldn't be allowed to go

14

to school. Learning things gives them ideas.

"Charlie," I began, "just think about it for a moment . . ."

And then Miss Wise said, "Dear me, Alex, you do seem to be in a chatty mood this morning. Why don't you go and sit next to Hélène for a bit? And at play time you can help me tidy up before you go out."

I spent the rest of the lesson frantically trying to signal *Don't be an idiot!* to Charlie without being seen by Miss Wise. But it was no use. By the time I'd carried all of Miss Wise's empty coffee mugs to the 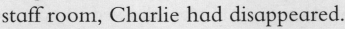 staff room, Charlie had disappeared.

He wasn't in the classroom; he wasn't in the playground. But I very quickly guessed where he would be.

The boys' toilets. If you're going to summon a Greek god from Mount Olympus it's best to find somewhere you're not likely to be disturbed by a teacher, and teachers don't usually come to the boys' toilets because they're a bit smelly. The toilets, that is, not the teachers. Even Mr Cameron, the school keeper, stays away from them if he possibly can.

I raced down the corridor towards the boys' loos. Running in the corridors is against the rules, but I didn't care. This was too important. If Charlie called Zeus back to school and Zeus came, there was no telling what he'd get up to. I almost leaped down the stairs and threw myself at the door.

I was too late. As I burst in, Charlie was saying, "Um, hello, Zeus. It's me. Charlie. I've made you this temple, and I dedicate it to you, OK?"

And just like that, Zeus appeared beside him, a big bearded man in an Ancient Greek tunic. "ABOUT TIME TOO!" he said, in the voice he used to impress people – which sounded even more boomy and echoey than usual in the toilets. "I've been wondering when you

17

two were going to build me a half-decent temple," he went on in his ordinary voice, looking around. Then he paused, and sniffed. "Why does it smell of wee?"

I sighed. "That's not the temple," I told him. "It's the toilets."

"This is the temple," Charlie said hopefully, holding it up.

Zeus stared at it. "I'm not having that," he said. "It's rubbish! It's even worse than one of Alex's!"

"But I made it specially!" Charlie said.

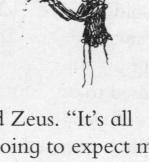

"Don't care," said Zeus. "It's all wrinkly. If you're going to expect me to appear for a rubbish temple like that, you could at least iron it first." He looked around. "I'd rather have the toilets. At least they won't go soggy in the rain."

"We can't dedicate the toilets to you!" I said. "They don't belong to us."

"Course they do," Zeus said. "They're the boys' toilets; you're boys. So they belong to you. That's logic, that is. The Greeks invented it, you know," he added proudly. "They knew what they were doing. *And* they didn't build temples that smelled of wee. Come on, High Priest, get dedicating."

I sighed again. There was no arguing with Zeus when he was in this sort of mood. And since "High Priest" meant me, I said, "Oh, great and mighty Zeus, I dedicate these toilets to be your temple. OK?"

"And, um, before you go . . ." Charlie began.

"Oh, right," Zeus said grumpily. "I might have known there'd be something else. Can't just dedicate me a temple without begging for favours, can you? What is it, then?"

Now that Zeus was here, I supposed there was no point in keeping it from him. "Charlie's being bullied," I told him.

"So what?" he said. "It's nothing to do with me. Anyway, it's probably not that bad, being bullied. I expect it builds character or something. He'll get over it."

"But—" Charlie began.

Zeus cut him off. "No!" he said. "You mortals are all the same – just 'me, me, me' all the time, expecting us gods to sort out your problems. You're selfish, that's your trouble."

"What about you, then?" I said. "Demanding sacrifices and temples and prayers without giving anything back. Isn't that selfish?"

"We're gods!" Zeus protested. "We're *supposed* to get sacrifices and temples and prayers. That's not selfish, that's just . . . that's just us getting stuff 'cos we want it! And talking of sacrifices – come on, let's have one before I go. You can't dedicate me a temple without making a sacrifice."

I shrugged. "I don't have anything to sacrifice."

Zeus scowled. "Course you do," he said. "Charlie's always got a play time snack, and he hasn't had time to eat it yet."

Charlie shook his head sadly. "Eric took it."

"Who's Eric?" Zeus demanded.

"The boy who's been bullying Charlie," I told him.

"Yeah, and every day he hits me, and trips me up, and steals my crisps," Charlie added. "And he scribbled on my card of you and gave you zero for power and wisdom and everything, and—"

"Hang on!" Zeus interrupted. "He defiled my image?"

"Did what?" Charlie asked.

"Scribbled on a picture of him," I said.

"Oh, yeah," said Charlie. "He did. And he tripped me up and hit me and—"

"And what do you mean, he gave me zero for power and wisdom?"

Charlie showed him the card. "He crumpled it too."

Zeus went red with anger, and little bolts of lightning began to

flash around
his forehead.
"That's . . . that's
sacrilege, that is!
Oooh, the little
creep! He can't
do that!"

card

"Yeah," Charlie
said, "and he hit me and tripped
me up and—"

"And ate my sacrifice before you'd
had time to sacrifice it?" Zeus cut in.

"I suppose so," I said.

"Yeah," Charlie agreed, "and he
hit me and tripped me up and flushed
my head in the toilet and knocked
me down and—"

"Yeah, yeah," Zeus said impatiently.
Then a thought seemed to strike him.
"Wait a minute! Which toilet?"

"That one," Charlie said, pointing.

"What – here? In my temple? He

came into my temple and flushed
someone's head in the toilet?"

"Yeah," said Charlie. "Mine."

"It doesn't matter whose head it
was," Zeus said irritably. "It's my
temple, *that's* the point!"

"It wasn't actually your temple
when he did it," I pointed out. "It was
just the boys' loo."

"That doesn't matter, though, does
it? It's my temple now! So what you're

saying is, this rotten kid defiled my image and disrespected my temple and gave me a score of nought for wisdom and power and strength and everything, and on top of all that he ate my sacrifice!"

"Yeah," Charlie said, "and he hit me, and tripped me, and—"

"Charlie," Zeus said with a sigh. "It's not all about you, you know."

"Oh," Charlie said. "Who is it all about, then?"

Zeus rolled his eyes. "Me, of course," he said. "Right; come on. Let's go and sort this kid out."

Chapter Three

The Twelve Labours of Heracles

We didn't go straight outside to sort
Eric out, because just then the bell
went and Zeus disguised
himself as a beetle like
he always did when he
came into class with
us. I was starting to get
used to having a Greek
god in my ear, but it still
tickled a bit.

mutter mutter

And it was still a bit annoying when
he kept muttering while I was trying
to listen to Miss Wise.

"Today, children," she was saying,
"we're going to learn about one of the

greatest of all the Greek heroes, and one a lot of you have probably heard of: Hercules."

"Call yourself a teacher?" grumbled Zeus, so quietly that only I could hear him. "You mean Heracles." He said it like *Heh-rah-klees*. "It was only those blinking Romans who called him Hercules. Typical of that lot: marching in where they weren't wanted, taking other people's gods and heroes and pretending they were theirs all the time . . ."

"Except," Miss Wise went on, "we're going to call him by his real name, the name the Greeks called him by: Heracles."

"Oh," Zeus said. "Right. That's all right, then."

It was a good story. Heracles was the strongest and bravest man in the world, but a god made him go mad for a bit, and while he was mad he killed his own children.

So then he had to be punished, even though it wasn't really his fault, and the punishment was that he had to be a king's slave until he'd done ten really hard jobs. And then after he'd finished, the king said he'd cheated at two of them, and made him do two more. Most of the labours – that was what they called the really hard jobs – would have made good stories by themselves, because they were about beating monsters. There were lots of other stories about him too, Miss Wise said – about how he strangled snakes when he was just a baby, and how he wrestled a river-god, and became a god himself after he died, and all kinds of other things.

The lesson was so interesting that by the end of it I'd almost forgotten I had a god in my ear. Which was a problem, because if Zeus was being quiet it probably meant he was planning something.

After the lesson we had lunch; and as soon as lunch was over we went back to the toilets – or, as Zeus insisted on calling them, his temple.

"Right," he said, changing back into his own shape as soon as we got there, "here's what we'll do. You take me out into the playground and show me this Eric kid, I'll smite him, and then I can go back to Mount Olympus and have a nice sit down and a cup of nectar."

"OK," said Charlie.

"No!" I said. "It's not OK! You

can't go around smiting people!"

"Yes he can!" Charlie argued. "If anyone deserves to get smitted, it's Eric!"

"Smitten, not smitted," I said, "and *nobody* deserves to get smitten."

"Yes, they do," said Zeus. "Anyway, it's an easy way to solve a problem. One minute there's a rotten kid going around eating my sacrifices and defiling my image, next minute there's a flash and a bang and a pair of smoking shoes. Hah! Nought out of ten for power, indeed! That'll show him!"

"Oh," said Charlie. "Is *that* what smiting means?"

"Of course!" Zeus said. "In the old days, I was always smiting people with thunderbolts. If I smote you, you stayed smitten. Once smitten, twice fried, that's what they used to say about my smitings—"

"Maybe," I interrupted, "but you can't go around smiting people in school. It's against the rules."

"Well, defiling my image and giving me nought out of ten and eating my sacrifices and flushing people's heads down the loos in my temple are all against *my* rules, Billy Bossyboots!" Zeus said crossly. "He can't do that sort of thing and get away

with it! I'm *going* to smite him, so there, and he'll know all about it! Well – he won't, actually. It'll all be over in a flash. That'll teach him."

"No, it won't," I pointed out. "If you smite him, he won't even *know* he's been smote — I mean, smitten. How can that teach him anything?"

Zeus thought about this. "I see what you mean," he said. "Maybe I ought to think of a different punishment — one that lasts a bit longer."

"You could send him to Tartarus," Charlie suggested, before I could stop him.

"Great idea!" Zeus said.

"Really?" Charlie asked. He doesn't often get told he's had a great idea. "Cool. How do we get him to Tartarus?"

"Easy," said Zeus. "First, I'll smite him —"

"Zeus!" I said. "We just agreed! No smiting!"

"All right," Zeus grumbled. "I don't *have* to smite him."

"Good," I said.

"I could just push him under a bus."

"No!" I said.

"All right, then," Zeus said. "*You* push him under a bus."

"No!" I said again.

Zeus sighed. "All right, all right. Charlie can push him under a bus."

"*No!*" I said. "Nobody's going to push anyone under a bus."

Zeus rolled his eyes. "Spoilsport," he said. "Poison, then."

"Zeus," I said. "*No!* Absolutely not! No killing of any sort!"

"Well, he can't go to Tartarus until he's dead, Clara Cleverclogs," Zeus said.

"Oh," said Charlie. "I didn't know that."

Neither did I. Maybe we should have worked a bit harder at our research.

"In that case," I said, "we can't send Eric to Tartarus. Miss Wise would get really cross if we killed anyone."

Charlie nodded. "She'd kill us," he said.

Zeus brightened. "Really?" he said. "Maybe we could get *her* to push him under a bus."

"He doesn't mean she'd *really* kill us," I explained. "He just means she'd get really really cross."

"Big deal," Zeus muttered. "Sounds like a rubbish punishment to me. Don't know what you're worried about that for."

"Anyway," I said, "the point is, nobody's going to kill anyone. You'll have to think of a different punishment."

But before he could say any more, I heard footsteps coming down the steps outside.

"Someone's coming!" I said to Zeus. "Hide!"

Zeus looked indignant. "I'm not going to hide in my own temple!" he said.

"It may be your temple," I told him, "but it's still the boys' toilets."

"What?!?" Zeus said. "You're not going to let people wee in my temple, are you?"

35

"I can't stop them!" I said. "What would the head teacher say if I told her the boys weren't allowed to go to the loo in school any more?"

"But it's *my temple!*" Zeus insisted.

The footsteps were getting closer. "You'll just have to share it!" I said. "Get out of sight! Quick!"

"Oh, all right," Zeus grumbled, and changed into a hamster – a grumpy,

muttering hamster that complained. "Honestly, the things I have to put up with these days," as it scuttled into one of the cubicles. "Not being allowed to smite anyone; having to let people wee in my temple; being given nought out of ten for wisdom and power. What next?" Grouchily, it shut the cubicle door.

Just in time, because the next moment the door into the loos opened with a bang. And my heart sank as I saw who was standing there, framed in the doorway.

It was Eric.

Chapter Four

Chapter Four

Eric

Eric was big – not just tall, but broad too, with a wide pink face. And just at that moment his wide pink face was wearing a look of gleeful meanness.

"Trying to hide again, are we, little Charlie?" he said. "Didn't anyone ever tell you how daft it is to hide in the same place twice?"

And he grabbed Charlie by the ear.

38

"Ow!" Charlie yelped. "Get off!"

"Leave him alone!" I said angrily.

Eric turned to me, sneering. "Make me," he said, grabbing my shirt with his other hand and shaking me, hard.

"Let go!" I yelled. "Stop it!"

There was a loud bang as the door to the cubicle burst open. There stood Zeus, his expression proud and regal and furious, drawn up to his full height and scowling ferociously at Eric. It would probably have been quite scary if he hadn't forgotten he was still a hamster.

"Cease this sacrilege, mortal!" he squeaked.

Eric stared at him in astonishment.

"Blimey!" he said. "A talking rat!"

Zeus looked down at his little furry paws. "Whoops," he muttered. Next second the hamster was gone and he towered over Eric in his own form. Lightning flashed wildly around his brow, and the sound of thunder echoed off the toilet walls.

"YOU DARE TO ENTER THE TEMPLE OF ZEUS AND LAY HANDS UPON HIS HIGH PRIEST!" he boomed angrily.

"THEN TREMBLE, MORTAL, BEFORE THE MIGHT OF ZEUS HIMSELF!!!"

Eric's mouth gaped with surprise. His eyes grew wide. He stared up at Zeus in startled amazement.

Then he said, "Eep!" and fainted.

Zeus rubbed his hands together happily. "Ha!" he said. "That showed him!"

"Yeah, thanks, Zeus," said Charlie. "That's taught him a lesson all right!"

"I don't think he'll be bothering Charlie again in a hurry," I agreed. "Thanks, Zeus. You can go and have that nice cup of nectar now."

Zeus looked at me in surprise. "Oh, no,"

41

he said. "Striking fear into his heart's only the first bit. I've got to punish him now."

I should have known it wouldn't be as easy as that.

"Don't you think scaring him so much he faints is punishment enough?" I asked.

Zeus shook his head firmly. "Nope," he said. "Not nearly. I need a really *good* punishment for him now. Hmmm ...let's see ..." He pulled distractedly at his beard, looking down at the unconscious Eric and thinking. "Who does he remind me of, lying there on his back like that?"

Suddenly, he snapped his fingers. "Got

it!" he said. "Prometheus!" He said it
like *Prom-ee-thee-us*. "I could do to him
what we did to Prometheus!"

"What was that?" Charlie asked.

"First," said Zeus, "we chained him
to a rock."

I didn't like the sound of this.

"Then we got
a big eagle to
come and eat
his liver."

"Eeeugh,"
said Charlie.
"Poor eagle."

"What do
you mean,
'poor eagle'?" Zeus demanded. "It
wasn't a punishment for the eagle."

"Sounds like one," Charlie said.
"Making it eat liver. Eeeugh."

"It didn't mind," Zeus said. "It
liked it."

"Oh," said Charlie. "It could come and eat mine, then, if it wanted."

"What?" I said.

"It could leave the bacon, though," he added.

"Charlie," I said, "what are you talking about?"

"Liver and bacon," Charlie said.

 "My dad cooks us liver and bacon every Monday, and I hate it. Well, the bacon's all right, but the liver's horrible. I wouldn't mind if an eagle came and ate it. Doesn't sound like much of a punishment to me, really. I should think Prometheus was quite pleased. Except for the bit about being chained to a rock."

"No, Charlie," I said, "it ate his actual liver. You know — *his* liver, inside him, like your heart and lungs and appendix and things."

Charlie went pale. "Oh," he said. "What happened then?"

"Then we made his liver grow back," Zeus said, "so the eagle had something to eat next day. It wouldn't have done to let it go hungry. That'd be cruel."

"Is he still there?" Charlie asked.

Zeus shook his head. "He got rescued after a few centuries. By Heracles, as it happens. Anyway, that's beside the point. Now, where can I get an eagle from?"

"There aren't any eagles round here," I told him.

"There are usually a few pigeons in the playground, though," Charlie said. "Mr Cameron says they're a right nuisance. He'd probably be quite pleased if you took them."

"We can't have his liver pecked out by pigeons!" Zeus said indignantly.

"We can't have his liver pecked out by anything," I said firmly. "He may be a bully, but he's only a kid. If you're going to punish him, it has to be a punishment for kids."

Zeus folded his arms crossly. "You're no fun," he muttered. "All right, then, smartypants: how do kids get punished round here?"

"Well," I said, thinking, "usually they get told off by a teacher. If it's really bad, they might have to go to the head teacher's office, or the deputy's."

"Big deal," said Zeus sarcastically. "Anyway, I can't see any of your teachers telling him off for sacrilege."

"Why don't *you* tell him off?"

Charlie suggested. "You could pretend to be a teacher."

Zeus stroked his beard again. "Hmmm . . . that might be fun," he said. "OK. I'll have to dress the part, though. What do teachers wear?"

"Miss Wise usually wears a dress," Charlie said.

"I meant *male* teachers," said Zeus.

"Oh," Charlie said. "We've only got one of those: Mr Cooper. He usually wears a tie. And he's always got leather patches on his elbows."

"What," said Zeus, "like this?"

I looked at the leather patches which had suddenly appeared on his elbows.

"Not quite like that," I told him. "I mean, the patches are fine, but Mr Cooper wears them on his jacket, not just stuck straight onto his arms."

"Oh," Zeus said; and suddenly he was wearing a jacket, too. "You mean like this?"

"Yes," I said, "like that. And the tie is usually multi-coloured, with a pattern on it."

"OK," Zeus said, and little flashes of lightning in red and yellow and green and blue began to appear all over his newly-materialised tie. "Great. I'll wake him up now. WAKE UP, YOU ROTTEN LITTLE CREEP!!!" he added, in his big booming voice.

"Hold on . . ." I began, but it was too late. Eric stirred, and groaned, and sat up before I had time to suggest to Zeus that a shirt and trousers might be a good idea as well.

"Where am I?" Eric murmured blearily.

"You're in my temple – I mean, office," Zeus told him.

Eric squinted bemusedly at him. "Why does it smell of wee?"

"Never mind that," Zeus said huffily. "The point is, you're in a lot of trouble, and I've got to decide on your punishment. Seeing as how I'm a teacher. A very important one, which is why I've got a temple. Office."

Eric was clearly very confused. "You don't look like a teacher," he said. "Why are you wearing a dress under your jacket?"

"It's not a dress, it's a tunic," Zeus said. "And I am so a teacher.

Why?

49

You can tell I'm a teacher, 'cos I've got elbow patches. On my elbows. Well, on my jacket's elbows. Though they could be on my actual elbows if I wanted. Anyway, that's not the point. What's your name?"

"Eric," said Eric, now completely bewildered.

"Eric what?" said Zeus.

"Eric, *sir*," Eric said.

"No, I mean – what's your last name?"

"Oh," Eric said. "It's Lees."

Zeus looked at him, and a big smile stretched across his face. "Really?" he said. "Eric Lees? Fantastic! That gives me a great idea for a punishment!"

Chapter Five

The Twelve Labours of Eric Lees

"Hang on," Eric said, getting up. "You can't punish me. I haven't done anything!"

"Oh, yes you have," said Zeus. "You've been a very naughty boy indeed."

"What've I done, then?"

Zeus folded his arms and glared down at Eric. "Do I really have to tell you?"

Eric folded his own arms and stared back. "It's not fair to punish me if I don't know what I'm supposed to have done."

Zeus tutted. "All right, Heracles –
I mean, Eric Lees. I'll tell you what
you've done wrong. You've killed
your children, that's what!"

Eric's mouth dropped open in

outraged surprise. "I never!" he said.

"Oh, yes you did!" Zeus said.

"No I never!" Eric repeated. "I
never killed anyone!"

"You did!" insisted Zeus. "You
killed your own children!"

"But I don't have any children!"
Eric protested.

"Course you don't!" Zeus said. "That's 'cos you've killed them all!"

"No," Eric said, "I mean, I never had any children in the first place!"

"Oh," said Zeus. "Are you sure?"

"Course I'm sure!" Eric said. "I'm only a kid! I'm too young to have children!"

"Oh," Zeus said again. "Well, I bet if you did have any children you'd have killed them. So now you have to be punished, and your punishment is—"

"Hang on!" Eric said. "You can't punish me for killing children I never had in the first place just 'cos you think I would have killed them if I'd had them!"

Zeus sighed. "Spoilsport," he said. "All right, then. How about if I punish you for sacrilege and blasphemy?"

"I don't even know what those are," Eric said.

"OK," Zeus said tetchily. "Well, you came into my temple – er, office, and grabbed hold of the High – I mean, Alex . . ."

"And me," Charlie said.

"Yeah, yeah, and Charlie," Zeus went on; "and another time you came into my . . . office, and flushed someone's head down the loo . . ."

"*My* head," put in Charlie.

"Yeah, yeah, Charlie's head," Zeus continued impatiently.

"Hang on!" Eric interrupted, looking round. "This isn't an office; it's the boys' toilets."

"It's the boys' toilets *and* my office, OK?" Zeus said crossly. "Now stop interrupting. And you scribbled on a card of m— of Zeus, and gave him nought for wisdom and power and stuff, and you stole my sacri— Charlie's crisps, and—"

"And hit me and tripped me up and called me names," Charlie said.

"All right, all right," Zeus said, "and you hit Charlie and tripped him up and called him names and killed your children. Didn't you?"

"Er . . . yeah, all right," admitted Eric. "I did, yeah. Except for the bit about killing my children," he added.

Zeus looked disappointed. I think re-enacting ancient Greek legends reminds him of the old days, when he had lots of worshippers, and he likes to get things as close to the original as he can.

"Anyway," he said, "the point is, you've done some bad things I can punish you for, haven't you?"

Eric nodded reluctantly.

"Right. So now you've got to do twelve labours."

"What?"

"Twelve labours. Twelve really hard jobs."

Eric stared at him. "That's not fair! That's twelve punishments!"

"Well," said Zeus, "it's supposed to be ten, really, but you'll probably cheat on two of them, so we might as well make it twelve right from the beginning."

"But it's not fair!" Eric said again.

Zeus shrugged. "I could always chain you to a rock and get an eagle to eat your liver," he said.

"I wouldn't mind," Eric said. "I don't like liver, anyway."

"No," said Zeus, "I mean . . . Oh, never mind. The point is, Eric Lees, that you've got to do twelve labours. All right?"

"All right," Eric said sulkily.

"Great!" Zeus said. "And the first one is . . . You must rid the land of the Nemean Lion!"

"*What?*" Eric said. "What mean lion?"

"Not *mean* lion," Zeus said. "*Nemean* Lion."

"And where am I going to find one of them?"

"Nemea, of course!" said Zeus, rolling his eyes. "You've got to go to Nemea, and find the Nemean Lion, and—"

Nemean Lion

"Hang on, hang on!" Eric protested. "Where's Nemea?"

"It's a bit of a distance," Zeus said. "You'd better get going."

This was getting out of hand. "Wait a minute, Zeu— er, Mr ..." I said, and then realized I didn't know what to call him in front of Eric.

"Mr King," Zeus said, with a big conspiratorial wink.

That made sense, I supposed. "Mr King," I went on, "you can't send him to Nemea. He'll miss school."

"I hadn't thought of that," Eric said. "Doesn't sound like such a bad idea to me."

 I glared at him, forgetting for a moment that glaring at the biggest, strongest, meanest and probably sneakiest kid in the school is a bad idea, even if you have got a Greek god on your side.

"Anyway," I added, "sending him outside the school grounds is against the rules. And teachers have to follow the rules."

Zeus pulled a face. "Spoilsport," he muttered again. "Well, how is he going to defeat the Nemean Lion if he can't go to Nemea? I mean, an ordinary lion would do, I suppose, seeing as he's just a kid, but if he can't even go outside the school grounds . . ."

"We could call the zoo and ask them to bring a lion here," Charlie suggested, not very helpfully. "And then he could try and defeat it."

"You're all bonkers!" Eric said. "How am I supposed to defeat a great big lion?"

"You could try flushing its head down the loo," Charlie said sarcastically.

"Not in my t — office," growled Zeus.

"Look," I said. "Real lions are out of the question – for much the same reason as smiting, poison, and shoving people under buses." Eric stared at me, more confused than ever, but I didn't care. "You'll just have to pick some other animal for him to defeat instead."

"Hmmmph," Zeus said sulkily. "What kind of animal are we going to find *inside* the school grounds that would do instead of the Nemean Lion?"

"Well," Charlie said hesitantly, "Mr Cameron's got a mean cat . . ."

Chapter Six

The First Labour, and Most of the Others

I'm not sure who was harder to convince – Eric, who kept moaning that having to fetch a cat wasn't a proper punishment and that he should just have been told off, or Zeus, who kept grumbling that fetching a cat wasn't a proper Labour and that there ought to be at least *some* danger of Eric getting killed. In the end, though, Eric went off to fetch the cat, and Zeus and Charlie and I discussed Eric's second task.

"Right," Zeus said, "the next one's the Hydra."

"What," said Charlie, "those things

firemen fix their hoses to?"

"That's a *hydrant*," I told him. "I don't think Heracles ever defeated one of those."

"I bet he could have if he'd wanted to," Charlie said. "What's a hydra, then?"

"Well," said Zeus, "it's kind of like a snake, but it's got nine heads. And if you cut one off, two more grow in its place. Oh," he added, "and it's deadly poisonous as well."

"Right," I said. "Well, there aren't many of those round here."

"I could probably get one from somewhere," Zeus suggested hopefully.

"I'd rather you didn't," I said. "What if Eric didn't defeat it and it killed everyone in the school?"

"I see what you mean," Zeus said. "There'd be nobody left to be my High Priest, and then where would my sacrifices come from? All right, what shall we tell him to defeat instead of a Hydra?"

We thought about it.

"Well," I said hesitantly after a while, "if you want him to defeat something wiggly and snake-like ..."

"Yes?" said Zeus.

"... that grows back when you cut it ..."

"Yes?" said Zeus, sounding very interested now.

"What about a worm?" I suggested.

"A *worm*?" Zeus exclaimed in disgust. "Oh, great! Terrific idea, you stupid High Priest! What kind of

Labour of Heracles is it to have to go out and defeat a worm? They're not exactly famous for their fighting skills, are they? I mean, how many people die of wormbite? How many people get injured because they can't move fast enough to evade a worm's lightning-fast reflexes? Eh? A worm, indeed! And it's not as if they grow two heads when you cut one off, is it?"

"No," I said, "but if you cut it in two in just the right place it grows another tail."

"Yes, but not straight away," Zeus pointed out. "What kind of hero is going to chop a worm in two and then hang around for days waiting for it to grow a new tail just so he can fight it some more?"

"Well, have you got a better idea?" I asked.

"Yeah," he grumbled. "I could smite the rotten little creep."

 Just then the door opened and Eric came in, cradling Mr Cameron's mean old cat in his arms and stroking it. He had a bit of a scratch on one hand, but seemed OK otherwise.

"Here we are," he said cheerfully. "That was easy, really. One cat, defeated. What's next?"

The cat, which had actually been pretty calm up until that moment, suddenly started wriggling. With a

hiss, a spit, and another scratch —
which made Eric go "Ow!" and drop
it — it was out of the door before it
had finished closing.

"What's up with it?" Charlie
wondered.

Eric shrugged. "Probably doesn't
like the smell," he said, sucking his
scratched hand. "Can't say I blame it.
Anyway — that's the first Labour done.
What's next?"

"Next, Eric Lees," said Zeus, casting
a glare in my direction, "for your
Second Labour, I command you to go
out and defeat . . . a worm!"

"A *worm*?" Eric repeated
incredulously.

"Yeah, it is a bit rubbish, isn't
it?" agreed Zeus. "Better make it a
bucketful of worms."

"How am I supposed to defeat
a bucketful of worms?" Eric said.

"Tickle them until they say '*I surrender*'?"

"You could just put them in a bucket," said Charlie.

"But I haven't got a bucket!" Eric objected.

"Well, it's not supposed to be flippin' well easy!" Zeus snapped. "It's a Labour! It's meant to be difficult! So go and get a bucket from somewhere and fill it with worms and bring it back here before I lose my temper and smite you!"

"You're not allowed to smite me," Eric said. "My mum says if a teacher smites me we can sue them."

Zeus stared at him and growled, a sound that echoed off the tiled walls like distant thunder.

"All right, all right," said Eric. "I'm going."

And he went.

"Right," said Zeus grumpily. "That should take him a few minutes. Let's work out the rest of the Labours."

"OK," I said. "What was Heracles's third one?"

"Let's see now . . ." Zeus rubbed his chin thoughtfully. "I don't think it was the bull . . . that came later. Oh, I know: he had to catch the Cerynian Hind."

"The what?" asked Charlie.

I remembered this one from Miss Wise's lesson. "It was a magic deer that could run really fast," I said. "It belonged to Artemis."

"Oh," said Charlie, pulling a face. "Her."

"So," Zeus went on, "we need to tell him to go and catch a fast animal . . ."

"But without going outside the school grounds," I reminded him. "And it can't be *too* fast. Heracles chased Artemis's hind for a year, but Eric's only got till the end of lunch time."

"You're no fun," Zeus grumped. "All right, then; for the Third Labour, he's got to go and catch, um . . ."

We thought for a bit. Eventually, Charlie said, "Well . . . there's always Mr Cameron's cat."

"But he's done the cat!" Zeus said. "What's the point in telling him to go out and do it again?"

"Um . . . it'll really annoy him?" Charlie said.

Zeus thought about this. "OK," he

said. "That might work. Now, for the Fourth Labour, Heracles had to defeat the Erymanthian Boar. I don't suppose you've got any ferocious boars in school?"

"Oh, yes we do!" Charlie said.

Zeus brightened. "Really?"

Charlie nodded. "There's Josh in our class, for one. He's always going on about where he's been on his holidays. Just goes on and on and on, blah blah blah, and won't talk about anything else. He's *really* boring. And then there's Mrs Henry. Everyone always falls asleep in her assemblies because they're so dull. And there's— What?"

Zeus was shaking his head crossly. "No," he said, "not *that* sort of bore. I mean a male pig."

"Oh," said Charlie. "Well ... Josh can be a pig as well. You should see the way he eats his lunch. And then —"

"No!" Zeus said. "I mean a *real* pig. What we need for the Fourth Labour is a fierce animal."

"Ah," Charlie said. "Like ... like Mr Cameron's cat?"

Zeus sighed. "All right," he said heavily.

"What's fifth?" I asked.

"Fifth is ..." he said. "Um ... fifth is ... Not the Mares of Diomedes ... Ooh, what is it again? Bother! I can't remember!"

"We can come back to it," I told him. "What about the others?"

The rest of the Labours, as far as Zeus remembered, were:

- Sixth: getting rid of the Stymphalian Birds, which had metal feathers and did poisonous poos and ate people
- Seventh: fetching the Cretan Bull, which was very fierce
- Eighth: fetching the Mares of Diomedes, which were man-eating horses
- Ninth: getting a belt from Hippolyta, Queen of some very fierce woman warriors called the Amazons
- Tenth: fetching the Cattle of Geryon, who was a monstrous giant
- Eleventh: fetching some Golden Apples from a place called the

Garden of the Hesperides, where they were guarded by a dragon with a hundred heads

- Twelfth: fetching Cerberus, the three-headed dog that guarded the gates of the kingdom of Hades, god of the dead

So, by the end of lunch time, Eric had:

- fetched a bucket of worms

- scared away the pigeons from the playground
- pinched a couple of leftover pieces of apple-cake from the school kitchens, which were guarded by the dinner-ladies, who are not the same as dragons but are probably nearly as fierce if you forget to say 'thank you'
- got a belt from Hippolyta – not Hippolyta the Queen of the Amazons, but Hippolyta Edwards in Eric's class, who is quite big and fierce. She wasn't wearing a belt, but when Eric called her "Fatty" she belted him right in the face, and Zeus, who was getting a bit fed up by this time, decided that that counted

- fetched Mr Cameron's cat seven times

"Right," said Eric grumpily, sucking at the scratches all over his hands and up his forearms.  "That's eleven. What's number twelve? You're not going to get me to fetch that blinking cat *again*, are you?"

Zeus still hadn't been able to remember the Fifth Labour. He was a bit cross at having to do that one out of the correct order; but then he was a bit cross anyway, about all the Labours of Eric Lees being a bit rubbish and nowhere near as good as the Labours of Heracles.

Luckily, just then the bell rang for the end of lunch time.

"You can do the last one after school," he said. "Come back here at the end of the day."

"OK," said Eric, and headed for the door. But just before he left – at a moment when Zeus wasn't looking at him – he glared ferociously at me and at Charlie. And it occurred to me that – no matter what the last Labour turned out to be – as soon as Zeus went back to Mount Olympus, Eric was going to make our lives a misery.

Chapter Seven

The Final Labour

It was games that afternoon, and Miss Wise took us all outside – all except Zeus, who stayed in the classroom in order to sneak a peek at *The Bumper Book of Greek Myths* and remind himself about the Labour he couldn't remember.

"Come to my temple after school," he muttered to me, before creeping out of my ear and hiding under the table. So at the end of the afternoon, Charlie and I went back to the boys' toilets to see what Zeus had come up with.

I was expecting him to be even

grumpier than before. My guess was
that the Fifth Labour was something
to do with defeating another fierce
animal, and that Zeus was going to
be all cross about having to tell Eric
to fetch Mr Cameron's cat again.
But when we
went in, Zeus
– back in the
jacket and
tie – was all
smiles.

"This," he
said, "is going
to be the best
Labour of all.
Better than all
the others put
together, and about a million times as
useful!"

"Why?" I asked. "What was the
Fifth Labour of Heracles?"

He grinned. "Cleaning out the Augean Stables!"

"The what?" Charlie asked.

"The stables of King Augeas," Zeus told him. "He kept loads and loads of cows in the stables and never ever cleaned them out, so they were full of about thirty years' worth of cattle-poo. Disgusting, it was. Heracles had to clean them out in a single day."

Charlie looked puzzled. "But we don't have any stables full of cow-poo," he said.

Zeus's grin got even bigger. "No," he said; "but we do have a temple that smells of wee!"

And just then, the door opened and Eric came in. He was holding Mr Cameron's cat, which looked pretty fed up by this time. It was already wriggling and struggling, and as soon as he got it inside it started spitting and scratching until he dropped it and it ran out again.

"Ow," he said bad-temperedly. "Right, I brought the cat again, and since I bet that was the last Labour I'll go home now, OK?"

"Oh, no you don't, Sally Smartypants!" Zeus said happily.

"That wasn't the last Labour at all!"

"Oh," said Eric. "Well . . . well, I've done it anyway, so shouldn't it count?"

Zeus shook his head. "Nope," he said. "If you want to go off doing extra Labours in your spare time, that's your business. But for your last proper Labour, Eric Lees, I command you to clean my temp — I mean, to clean my office until it doesn't smell of wee any more!"

Eric's face fell. "What?" he said. "But . . . but that'll take *ages*!"

"Better get started, then," Zeus told him cheerily.

Eric folded his arms and gazed at Zeus, a sudden look of cunning on his face. "Hang on. This is the last Labour, right?" he said.

"Yup!" said Zeus.

"And once I've done this one, I'm in the clear?"

Zeus nodded. "That's right!"

"And I can do it any way I want to?"

"Any way at all," agreed Zeus. "As long as you get rid of the smell, you can do it however you want."

"Right," Eric said. "Maybe it won't take so long after all!"

He went over to the nearest tap, held his thumb over the spout, and turned it on. A jet of water shot out, hitting Zeus right in the face.

"Oi!" Zeus yelled.

"Sorry!" Eric said, in a sing-song voice that meant he wasn't sorry at all. He twisted his thumb, aiming the jet of water until most of it was spraying right at the urinal, hosing it down – although it was also squirting out sideways and upwards too, and making a bit of a mess.

I looked at Zeus, expecting him to be furious, but despite the water dripping off his beard he looked pretty calm. More than that, in fact, he looked slightly amused.

"I wouldn't do that if I were you," he said.

"You said I could do it any way I wanted," Eric said cheekily, leaving the first tap running and moving on to the next. "Well, I want to do it this way."

Zeus shrugged. "Suit yourself," he said.

And then I realized something. The

little lightning bolt that Zeus once gave me, which I wear around my neck on a chain, was tingling against my skin. This was a bit worrying; the last time it did that, it turned out to be a warning about the new girl in my class. But this couldn't be a warning about Eric; he'd been at the school longer than I had, and the lightning bolt had never tingled near him before. So I wasn't sure what it might mean, but I guessed it might not be good.

Eric did some more squirting with the next tap, and the next, and the tingling got stronger and stronger. The floor was soaking, and so were the walls. It did seem as if the smell wasn't quite as bad now, though.

Encouraged, Eric went back to the first tap and squirted with it again, and then moved on to the second, and so on, down the line, until he'd done the same thing twice with each one.

It was when he went back to the first tap for the third time that it happened.

He'd just closed his thumb over the spout again when an angry voice shouted, "Right! That's *it*!"

Eric looked round in confusion, wondering who had spoken. Actually, Charlie and I were wondering the same thing. It hadn't been any of us, and it hadn't been Zeus. In fact, even though we were in the boys' loos, the voice that had spoken was quite definitely a girl's.

"Let go!" the voice yelled, and next second a girl, wearing a tunic like Zeus's, stepped out of the spray. Eric's eyes bulged in disbelief.

"What do you think you're doing, squirting my water at that disgusting trough?" the girl scolded, advancing on Eric.

"Er ... er ..." Eric spluttered, lost for words.

"Who's that?" Charlie asked, gaping.

"Her?" Zeus said.

"She's a naiad."

"A what?" Charlie said.

I remembered this one from Sophie and Leah's research that morning. "A water-nymph," I said. "The ancient Greeks believed there was a spirit in every stream and fountain and well."

"And tap?" Charlie said.

"It looks like it," I agreed. And it did, for now there were girls standing in every basin, their ankles in the streams from the running taps, all of them glaring at Eric.

"Why not?" Zeus said. "If it's running water, it ought to have a naiad. It's only fair."

"And do these naiads live here?" I asked. "All the time?"

"Of course they do!" Zeus said.

"What – in the boys' loos?" Charlie asked, scandalized. "But they're *girls*!" His mouth dropped open as another thought struck him: "Do you mean . . . they can *see* us when we come in and . . . *eeeugh!*"

Zeus nodded thoughtfully. "It's the naiads in the toilet flushes I feel really sorry for," he said.

"Blimey," said Charlie. "No wonder they look so cross!"

And they did. As we watched, each naiad jumped gracefully but threateningly down from her basin and advanced upon Eric.

"Well?" the first one said. "It's bad enough having to live here all the time, having our lovely clean water used to wash dirty hands, without you

squirting it at that smelly
... that smelly *thing* over
there!"

"I was just ... I was just
trying to clean it!" Eric
spluttered. "It's a Labour!
I've got to get rid of the
smell, you see, and ..."

"Oh, I see," said another naiad.
"Well, we can help you with that,
can't we, girls?"

"You can?" Eric said nervously.

"Oh, yes," said a third. "All it needs
is a good scrub!"

And with that, they grabbed him.
Eric yelled and screamed in protest,
and struggled and kicked, but there
were too many of them, and within
seconds they had lifted him off the
ground and were scrubbing away at
the urinal with him, using him like a
great big sponge.

"Oi! Stop! Stop!" Eric begged, but it was no use; they scrubbed and scrubbed until the urinal was cleaner and more sparkling than it had ever been – and Eric was soggy and smelly and wretched. Then they set him down on the floor, and Eric Lees – the biggest, meanest, nastiest kid in the school – burst into tears and ran out.

And Zeus, Charlie and I burst out laughing.

Chapter Eight

The Dedication of the Temple

The naiads bowed gracefully to Zeus, climbed back into the basins, and disappeared into the streams of running water. Carefully and respectfully, Charlie and I turned the taps off again.

Zeus looked enormously pleased

with himself. "Well," he said, "that's sorted *him* out. He won't be giving *me* nought out of ten for wisdom and power and stuff in a hurry!"

"Or flushing my head down the loo," Charlie added.

I wasn't so sure. But before I could say anything, Zeus went on: "So I'll be off, then." He looked around. "It's good to have a nice clean temple made of proper bricks and things again. Which reminds me, Mr High Priest" – and here he looked at me – "you need to finish dedicating it!"

"What do you mean?" I said. "We did that this morning!"

He shook his head. "You prayed a prayer of dedication," he said, "and a pretty rubbish prayer it was, though I suppose it'll have to do; but you haven't done the sacrifice yet."

"Oh," I said. "That."

"Yes," he said, "that. And none of your ordinary little poky day-to-day sacrifices, buster – this one's got to be big and special. It's not every day I get a new temple dedicated to me. Although," he added, "now that you've got a proper temple to do them in – or at least one that won't go all wrinkly and collapse in a matter of days – you can start doing proper morning sacrifices!"

"What," I said, "every day?"

He grinned. "Yep," he said. "Or at least, every day that school's open. Starting with the dedicatory sacrifice tomorrow. Don't forget!"

With that, he was gone. Our worries, though, were far from over.

As we left the school, we saw Eric squelching his way home slowly. And he saw us.

"You two better watch out!" he

shouted tearfully, shaking his fist at us from the opposite side of the road.

"When that Mr Whatsisname's not around, I'll get you! I'll get you, and you'll be sorry! You think this is bad? It's nothing to what I'm going to do to you two!"

Charlie stuck his tongue out at him.

"Charlie!" I said, "don't be an idiot! You heard what he just said!"

"Yeah," said Charlie, "but he's too wet to run after us."

"He is now," I pointed out. "He

won't be tomorrow."

Charlie's face fell. "I hadn't thought of that," he said.

"Well, you'd better," I told him. "He's going to blame us for everything that's happened: the Labours, the naiads, Zeus – everything."

"But that's not fair!" Charlie objected. "Why would he blame us for all that?"

I thought of saying, *Well, it was your fault in a way. You were the one who called Zeus when I told you not to.* But that wouldn't really have been fair, either. So I just said, "Because we're smaller than him; and we were there. And because he's a bully, and that's what bullies are like."

And then we said goodbye at the

end of Charlie's street, and I went
home and worried all evening.

It turned out I needn't have worried
at all. Charlie and I walked to school
together the next day, and we were
nowhere near the school gates when
we heard the shouting.

  As we got nearer, we could see
a huge crowd of children in the
playground, all gathered around Miss
Wise, and a big cross lady who was
holding Eric by the hand.

"Really, Mrs Lees," Miss Wise was saying, but Eric's mum was just shouting and shouting and not letting her speak.

And then the head teacher came out. "Now, then, Mrs Lees," she said, "what seems to be the trouble?"

"I'll tell you what seems to be the trouble!" Eric's mum screeched. "You've got a teacher here who's a loony, and I want him sacked! Now!"

"Mr Cooper?" said the head, trying to calm the irate woman down.

Mr Cooper

"I'm sure there must be some mistake ..."

"I don't know what his name is," yelled Mrs Lees, purple with fury, "but he wears a jacket with elbow patches ..."

"Well, that *sounds* like Mr Cooper," the head said.

". . . and a white dress!"

There was a pause while Mrs Lees drew breath. The head stared at her. "A *dress*? No, I can assure you that Mr Cooper has never worn a dress to school . . ."

But Mrs Lees was off again. "And he's got his office in the boys' loos, and he keeps a gang of violent girls in the taps!"

"In the *taps*?" the head said. "An office in the boys' toilets? Mrs Lees, are you sure you're feeling quite well?"

"There's nothing wrong with me!" Mrs Lees shouted. "But your Mr Whatsisface needs locking up! Punishing my little Eric, who's never done a thing wrong in his life, by making him fetch cats and worms, and pinch cake from the kitchens, and—"

"Oh," interrupted the head rather more coldly. "Was it *Eric* who stole those pieces of cake yesterday?"

"Only 'cos he was made to!" the furious Mrs Lees ranted. "And then he was used as a scrubbing-cloth to clean the toilets! I know my rights! If you don't give that blinking teacher the sack this minute, then—"

"Mrs Lees," the head said, "wherever did you hear this extraordinary story?"

"From my little Eric, of course," she declared, patting Eric – who, stiff and red with embarrassment, looked almost as if he was trying to hide behind her. "He came home last night, soaking wet, and told me all about it!"

"And has it occurred to you," the

head asked, "that perhaps your little Eric might not have been . . . entirely truthful?"

Mrs Lees's mouth dropped open as if she had been slapped. "Are you calling my Eric a liar?" she demanded.

"Well," the head began, "if he told you that a male teacher who wears a dress and has his office in the boys' toilets and keeps a gang of violent girls in the taps made him fetch cats and worms and steal cake as a punishment for doing nothing wrong, then perhaps you might think—"

"I'm not thinking anything!" Mrs Lees fumed. "If my little Eric says it, it must be true; and if you're going to call him a liar then this is clearly not the right school for him! Come along, Eric!" she added, still at full volume. "We'll find you a better school!"

Without further ado, and dragging

Eric behind her, she stormed off through the school gates and away.

And the whole school broke into applause.

"Now, children," the head said, making a sort of *Calm down* sign with her hands, "let's not be unkind." But we could see she was quite pleased, really.

Charlie and I were pleased too; and I was glad I'd bought the biggest bag of the poshest Roast Beef and Mustard flavour crisps I could find for the dedicatory sacrifice. Which Charlie and I rushed off to do.

"Oh, great and mighty Zeus," I said as I opened the bag, "I sacrifice this family-sized bag of Roast Bull-flavoured crisps . . ."

"With mustard," Charlie put in.

"With mustard," I agreed. "I sacrifice it to you in honour of the dedication of your new temple, and hope you enjoy it. And I hope you don't mind, but I've brought something for the naiads too," I added. "Just to say thanks." I got out a bag of prawn cocktail flavour – I thought they might like something a bit more fishy – and put a crisp under each tap, turning on the water until all the flavouring was washed away.

"Oh, and Zeus," Charlie added, as we opened the door to leave, "thanks for sorting Eric out."

And as the door closed behind us we heard a noise which could have been a distant, god-like chuckle. Or perhaps it was just the water gurgling through the pipes.